Defoe Abbott Marx Hardy Melville Machiavelli Montaigne Haggard Chesterton Cooper Emerson Joyce Austen Hugo Eliot Grimm
Stoker Carroll Christie Maupassant Byron Engels Schiller Moliere
Wilde Garnett Goethe Einstein Fitzgerald Hawthorne Smith Kafka Hall
Baum Cotton Henry Dostoyevsky Kipling Doyle Willis
Leslie Dumas Flaubert Turgenev Balzac
Stockton Vatsyayana Crane
Burroughs Verne
Curtis Tocqueville Whitman Gogol Vinci
Homer Widger Tolstoy Busch
Darwin Thoreau Twain Scott Harte Plato
Potter Freud Zola Lawrence Dickens Burton Hesse
Kant Jowett Stevenson Cervantes
Andersen Voltaire
London Descartes Cooke
Poe Aristotle Wells Irving
Hale James Hastings
Bunner Shakespeare
Richter Chambers Alcott
Doré Dante Chekhov da Shaw Benedict Pushkin
Swift Wodehouse Newton

 tredition®

tredition was established in 2006 by Sandra Latusseck and Soenke Schulz. Based in Hamburg, Germany, tredition offers publishing solutions to authors and publishing houses, combined with world-wide distribution of printed and digital book content. tredition is uniquely positioned to enable authors and publishing houses to create books on their own terms and without conventional manufacturing risks.

For more information please visit: www.tredition.com

TREDITION CLASSICS

This book is part of the TREDITION CLASSICS series. The creators of this series are united by passion for literature and driven by the intention of making all public domain books available in printed format again - worldwide. Most TREDITION CLASSICS titles have been out of print and off the bookstore shelves for decades. At tredition we believe that a great book never goes out of style and that its value is eternal. Several mostly non-profit literature projects provide content to tredition. To support their good work, tredition donates a portion of the proceeds from each sold copy. As a reader of a TREDITION CLASSICS book, you support our mission to save many of the amazing works of world literature from oblivion. See all available books at www.tredition.com.

Project Gutenberg

The content for this book has been graciously provided by Project Gutenberg. Project Gutenberg is a non-profit organization founded by Michael Hart in 1971 at the University of Illinois. The mission of Project Gutenberg is simple: To encourage the creation and distribution of eBooks. Project Gutenberg is the first and largest collection of public domain eBooks.

Sonny Boy

Sophie Miriam Swett

Imprint

This book is part of TREDITION CLASSICS

Author: Sophie Miriam Swett
Cover design: Buchgut, Berlin – Germany

Publisher: tredition GmbH, Hamburg - Germany
ISBN: 978-3-8472-1248-5

www.tredition.com
www.tredition.de

SONNY
BOY
—
SOPHIE
SWETT
ALTEMUS
SONNY
BOY
SOPHIE SWETT

Sonny Boy

Sonny Boy

By

Sophie Swett

Author of "Mary Augusta's Price," etc.

Illustrated

PHILADELPHIA

HENRY ALTEMUS COMPANY

By the Same Author

MARY AUGUSTA'S PRICE

Price, Fifty Cents

A GREAT SURPRISE FOR THE PLUMMERS

13

SONNY BOY

CHAPTER I

A GREAT SURPRISE FOR THE PLUMMERS

Mamma Plummer read a letter at the dinner-table before she touched her soup. She had been having visitors and had not had time to look at it before. And she was always in a hurry to hear from Aunt Kate.

Aunt Kate! All seven of the young Plummers pricked up their ears.

Aunt Kate was "the right kind," as Tom Plummer said. She remembered all the young Plummers' birthdays, and even when she was in Europe 14 sent home beautiful presents that arrived in Poppleton on the very day. A present is so much better on the very day.

"Aunt Kate is lonesome, in her new house, without any young people," said Mamma Plummer, at last. "She wants to borrow one of you children for six months."

There was a chorus of delight from the young Plummers. Mamma Plummer sighed a little. People were always saying, "How many there are of the Plummers," but Mamma Plummer never thought there were too many.

"Probably she wants one of us," whispered Dorothy, who was sixteen, to Polly, who was eighteen.

Sydney, who was fifteen, waited eagerly. He thought Aunt Kate might have heard of the picture on 15 the barn door and mean to give him a chance to become a great artist. Any one could see that the picture meant a man on horseback, with a pipe in his mouth, and that the man was Michael, their gardener, even if Tom did pretend to think it was the town pump.

Oliver stood up on a round of his chair; he was short, and he had such a little, squeaky voice that he had to get up high to make people notice him.

"She *may* want one of the youngsters," said Polly doubtfully. "She said Trixie was a quaint child."

"I'm not a quaint child," said Trixie, as if her feelings were hurt. "And I'm not the one who can leave home just as well as not. So many things disagree with Bevis, and the Bantam rooster pecks my chicks." 16

"You sha'n't go," said Papa Plummer, patting her head. They all knew that Trixie was a home body. Once, when she tried to stay at Aunt Sarah's, they had to bring her home in the middle of the night.

"If she wants me," said Tom, "I'm her man." But Tom was eating his dinner just as if nothing had happened.

Tom was twelve, and had learned that you can't have everything you want in this world, and that the things you get sometimes turn out better than the things you want and can't get.

Another one of the Plummers was quietly eating his dinner. That was because he was sure that Aunt Kate didn't want him. None of the others had even thought of Sonny Boy. It was a matter of course, they would 17 have said, that Aunt Kate didn't want Sonny Boy.

Sonny Boy was ten. His name was Peter, but Mamma thought that too large a name for a small boy. Besides, there was another Peter Plummer—his cousin—who lived on Pippin Hill. Both Peters were named for Grandpa Plummer.

All the other Plummers were handsome, but Sonny Boy was snub-nosed and freckled and a trifle cross-eyed, and his curly hair was so red that the boys pretended to warm their hands and light matches by it. He had stooping shoulders, too, and perhaps his legs bowed a little.

And he was not very bright at his lessons, while all the other Plummers *were* bright.

So, except his mother and grandmother, people didn't think so very 18 highly of Sonny Boy, though they liked him well enough, and he was very often left out of good times.

Sonny Boy ate his dinner and only thought that the one who was borrowed by Aunt Kate would be pretty lucky. He thought it would be Polly, and he rather hoped so, for Polly always thought he would better be sent to bed early when there was company.

"Mamma Plummer! Please decide who is to go and not keep us waiting!" cried Polly eagerly.

"Your Aunt Kate has decided which one she wants," said Mamma Plummer. And then her glance wandered down the long table and rested wonderingly, although lovingly, just where one would have least expected.

"Aunt Kate wants Sonny Boy," she said. 19

"Sonny Boy!" echoed all the young Plummers in a chorus of astonishment. Every one of them could see plenty of reasons why Aunt Kate should want him or her, but not a single reason why she should want Sonny Boy to stay with her six months.

Sonny Boy blushed red with surprise, and then he blushed redder with delight, and then reddest of all because everybody was looking at him.

And then he stole a glance at Mamma and at Grandma. The first thing is, you know, to be sure that those you love best are glad with you. Then Sonny Boy whispered to Tom.

"If you wanted to go, Tom, I'd stay," he said.

"Naw-w," said Tom, with the contempt of one who has not been invited. 20

"Or if you thought they'd let me belong to the Company, I'd rather stay home and belong than to go to Aunt Kate's," added Sonny Boy.

Tom was one of the boys who were getting up a company of soldiers, but Sonny Boy had never dared to say before that he wanted to join it.

Tom laughed aloud. "A great soldier you'd make, Sonny Boy! The fellows wouldn't want you to belong," he said.

Tom didn't mean to be unkind, but he thought that when a boy was rather bow-legged and never had got out of the small school, he ought to know that he wasn't cut out for a soldier.

"It's well enough for him to go and visit his Aunt Kate," thought Tom.

"'AUNT KATE WANTS SONNY BOY,' SHE SAID."

"You must remember not to give Bevis pound-cake when I'm gone," said Sonny Boy, looking very cross-eyed indeed at Trixie, as he always did when he had a good deal on his mind. And surely to go away from home, suddenly, for six months, is a good deal for any person to have on his mind! 25

SONNY BOY GOES ON A JOURNEY AND MAKES FRIENDS

27

CHAPTER II

SONNY BOY GOES ON A JOURNEY AND MAKES FRIENDS

Sonny Boy set out, all alone, for the city in which Aunt Kate lived. Papa Plummer thought that any kind of a boy of ten ought to be able to make a little journey like that alone.

The whole Plummer family went with Sonny Boy to the Poppleton station and gave him charges, while they waited for the train. "Write every day," said Mamma Plummer, "and learn to spell, and don't touch Aunt Kate's scissors to your curls."

"Say your prayers," whispered 28 Grandma Plummer, "and change your wet feet."

"Don't lose your money," said Papa Plummer.

"Eat your soup from the side of the spoon, and don't say 'ain't' nor 'is that so,'" said Polly, in a severe tone.

"Don't scuff nor speak through your nose, and don't say 'No-sir-ee' to Aunt Kate," said Dorothy.

"If you go to the circus that was here last summer, find out whether the Wild Man is truly wild," said Tom, "and see what a big drum costs—big enough for the Company."

"Go to a dog-man and find out what is good for Bevis' dyspepsia, and whether he may eat cookies," said Trixie.

And then the train came whizzing along, and, with his cage of white 29 mice under his arm, and his turtle sticking its head out of his jacket pocket, Sonny Boy went into the car.

As the train moved off Sonny Boy shut his teeth tight together. In his heart he was afraid he should be homesick, like Trixie.

He took the paper off the cage to give his white mice the air, and a woman in the seat behind jumped and screamed.

"Oh, take them away! Take them away! They'll get out!" she cried. "Anyway, they'll frighten my baby into fits!"

Then immediately the conductor came along and angrily told Sonny Boy that that wasn't a menagerie car, and he must either throw those things away or carry them into the baggage-car. He said some people with a screeching parrot were out in the baggage-car. 30 They would not trust their parrot there alone, and people in the cars wouldn't hear it screech.

Sonny Boy, with a very red face, followed the conductor to the baggage-car.

On a trunk a little girl was sitting, with her nurse, a rather cross-looking woman, beside her. Between them was a large cage. "If you want to leave your live stock here, you can go back to the car. I guess 'twill be safe enough," said the conductor. But Sonny Boy shook his head firmly.

"Oh, what lovely little dears!" cried the little girl. She was about as old a little girl as Trixie, but she had a bright, grown-up manner that made Sonny Boy feel bashful.

"Pussy? Pussy? Scat!" shrieked the parrot from the little girl's cage.

33

"Isn't Polly wonderful to know that they are mice?" cried the little girl to Sonny Boy.

But the mice, not being used to pussies, did not mind hearing her call a cat in the least.

Some were quietly nibbling at a lump of sugar which Trixie had put into the cage for them, and some were trying to thrust their heads through the wires to see the world.

"Polly is a gray African parrot," said the little girl. "She knows a lot, and she's worth a hundred dollars. We are carrying her to Otto, at the hospital, but we are a little afraid they won't let him keep her there, for some don't like her voice."

"I like it," said Sonny Boy, politely and truthfully.

"So do I like your mice," said the little girl as politely. 34

And then they felt they had known each other for a long time.

They sat down on a large trunk, with the cage of mice between them, and Sonny Boy told the little girl that the mice with black spots on them were Spaniards, and showed her just which of the white ones were Dewey and Sampson, and told her that the dashing little fellow that led all the others in daring swings and leaps was Hobson.

"Oh, if Otto could only see them!" cried the little girl. "He loves soldiers. He wants to be one, and only think! he isn't like other boys. His back isn't straight and he is lame, and though he is eleven you wouldn't think him more than eight."

To be lame was worse than to be bow-legged, and Sonny Boy felt a thrill of pity for Otto. He hoped 35 Otto wasn't cross-eyed, and he quite longed to ask if fractions and spelling came hard to him.

When it was nearly dark the nurse said that the next stopping-place would be their station, and she put a newspaper over the parrot's cage and made ready to leave the car.

The train would reach the city soon after it left their station, she said, so Sonny Boy covered his mouse-cage with a newspaper, too, and prepared to say good-bye to his new friend.

There was great hurry and bustle when Lena and her nurse reached their station, but Lena ran back after she had gone down the car steps to tell Sonny Boy that he was one of the nicest boys she had ever seen, and had been beautifully kind all the afternoon to her and to her nurse. Sonny 36 Boy wished that Polly could have heard her!

In the great city station Aunt Kate's big, pompous coachman came shouting through the crowd for "Master Peter Plummer." And Sonny Boy had to stop to think who it was he meant, for in Poppleton he was never called anything but Sonny Boy.

"Take your things, sir?" said the pompous footman, just as if Sonny Boy were grown up!

"I'll take this, please," said Sonny Boy, keeping hold of the cage. "It's full of white mice."

"Dewey! Sampson! Hobson! Cock-a-doodle-doo! Pussy! Pussy! Scat! Polly wants a cracker!" cried a shrill voice from the cage. And the pompous coachman stared in amazement.

"HE TOLD HER WHICH WERE SPANIARDS."

"It's Lena's parrot! We must have changed cages! Oh, and she's got my white mice!" cried Sonny Boy. 41

SONNY BOY

GOES IN SEARCH OF HIS

WHITE MICE

43

CHAPTER III

SONNY BOY GOES IN SEARCH OF HIS WHITE MICE

"My dear Sonny Boy!" Aunt Kate leaned out of her carriage, ready to take him, big cage and all, into her arms.

"Cock-a-doodle-doo! Remember the Maine! Dewey! Sampson! Hobson!" screamed the parrot again. And the crowd following Sonny Boy and the coachman cheered and cheered.

Sonny Boy was afraid they would tear the cage from his arms. And they might have, had not the coachman used his fists to clear the way. 44

"Get us out of this, Jarvis!" said Aunt Kate.

Jarvis made the horses plunge forward, but Sonny Boy could hear the shouts following them along the street.

"She—she's a remarkable parrot," said Sonny Boy faintly.

"I should think so!" said Aunt Kate.

"I didn't exactly bring the parrot. She belongs to another fel—another girl," explained Sonny Boy, a little confused.

"I'm so glad!" said Aunt Kate heartily.

"I had my white mice in a cage just about as large as this. You ought to see them! Trixie and I have drilled them into two armies, American and Spanish, and we've got the commanders on both sides—and, oh, I don't know where they are now! I changed cages with a girl!"

47

"Oh, we'll find them, never fear! And the girl shall have her parrot," said Aunt Kate, growing suddenly very cheerful.

When they reached Aunt Kate's house a beautiful Angora cat ran into the hall to meet her mistress. "Scat! Scat!" screamed the parrot. She had torn the newspaper off the cage with her sharp beak and was taking a look around her.

Off whisked the cat in terror, and hid, so that no one could find her. Then Aunt Kate's little poodle waddled up to the cage. "Bow-wow!" barked the parrot. And they couldn't drag the poodle out of the coal-cellar that night!

Sonny Boy lay awake that night longer than he had ever lain awake 48 a night in his life, planning how to rid himself of that parrot and get his white mice again.

In the morning Aunt Kate sent out for all the daily papers, but there was no advertisement of a lost parrot in them. The parrot, with her cage muffled, was shut up in the back attic, but Aunt Kate had a nervous headache.

Sonny Boy felt sure that she was wishing she had borrowed some other one of the Plummers who wouldn't have brought a parrot, and he was very unhappy. When Aunt Kate sat down at her desk to write an advertisement for a girl who changed a parrot for a cage of white mice, Sonny Boy stole up to the attic and got the parrot, and slipped out at the front door. He did not know the name of the station where Lena and her nurse had stopped, but he knew that it was 49 the next station to the city, and that there was a children's hospital there.

When Aunt Kate had said they couldn't find the little girl without advertising, as they did not know her last name, Sonny Boy had been too bashful to tell her he thought he could.

But of course any little Poppleton boy knew what tongues were made for, and Sonny Boy felt he could make things come out right if that parrot would only keep still!

He had learned the way to the station and was hurrying on when a newsboy's cry about the war aroused Polly.

She shouted all her war-cries, and such a crowd gathered that Sonny Boy was forced to turn into a side street and run.

But fortunately the side street led 50 to the station, and once on board the train Polly became quiet.

He got out at the station where Lena had left him, the day before, and inquired for the children's hospital.

There was no children's hospital, he was told, but there was a children's ward in the big general hospital on the hill, which the station-agent pointed out to him.

He rang timidly at the great door of the hospital, then waited a long time.

"Hurry up! Hurry up!" shrieked Polly. And a man, looking very much astonished, opened the door.

"I want to see a boy named Otto," said Sonny Boy. "I want to give him his parrot and—"

"Are you his brother?" asked the man. "Only relatives admitted." And when Sonny Boy shook his head he shut the door.

"'ARE YOU HIS BROTHER?' ASKED THE MAN."

"Cock-a-doodle! Remember the Maine!" screamed Polly.

The man opened the door enough to look at the parrot.

"Please won't you see if Otto has my white mice?" urged Sonny Boy.

"His sister is here. You might send for her to come out," said a boy in buttons at the man's elbow.

The great door was closed again, but in a few moments it opened and Lena's startled face appeared.

"I didn't do it on purpose," she said, her cheeks growing very red. "But I did hope you would like her better, for Otto is just wild over the mice!"

"I don't like her better!" said Sonny Boy stoutly.

"We think Otto ought to have 54 everything. When you see him you'll think so, too," said Lena.

"I sha'n't think he ought to have my white mice," said Sonny Boy firmly.

The girl opened wide the big door, as if it belonged to her.

"Come!" she said, beckoning to Sonny Boy. 55

SONNY BOY

FINDS A CROOKEDER BOY

57

CHAPTER IV

SONNY BOY FINDS A CROOKEDER BOY

Sonny Boy followed Lena through the great door.

The doorkeeper said if he was a friend of hers he might go in for a little while, but the parrot must be kept outside; she was too noisy.

The boy in buttons seemed very willing to take care of Polly. He said he would carry her out upon the grounds and give her an airing.

Lena led Sonny Boy into a large, long room, which she said was the "almost well" room of the children's ward.

"But we're afraid Otto never will be well," she whispered, turning a sad 58 little face toward Sonny Boy, as she opened the door.

"Otto, the mice boy has come to see you!" she said to a white-faced, humpbacked boy, who sat propped up in a chair, at a table, with the cage of mice before him.

The boy drew the cage towards him and placed his thin white hands over it.

"Have you come for them?" he asked, with a sob in his throat.

"Let me show you what they will do!" said Sonny Boy, and sat down opposite him at the table.

Those mice had been trained before Sonny Boy had them, and for two years he and Tom and Trixie had been teaching them. When either of the young Plummers had the mumps or the measles, or there was a long storm, it meant several new tricks for the white mice! and they could now do really wonderful things.

"'LET ME SHOW YOU WHAT THEY WILL DO.'"

61

Since the war with Spain had begun, they were taught soldier tricks altogether. And it was so fortunate that some had black spots, for those could be Spaniards!

All the children in the ward who could walk crowded around the table, and the matron and the nurses, too.

It was such a good time that many an ache and pain was forgotten for many minutes. When Sonny Boy let the mice out of the cage and they scampered all over the table, then the children scampered, too—every one who could. Even the matron and the nurses uttered little screams.

But Sonny Boy whistled, and into the cage marched those mice like soldiers! It was really a wonderful sight to see. 62

And the worn and tired looks were gone from so many children's faces!

Otto's poor, shrunken, misshaped body shook with laughter. "I want to know how you trained them!" he said. "I want to train them! I want to do everything that well boys do—that you do! And I'm going to learn! Lena is only a girl, and I never had a brother. I think I could even learn spelling and fractions if you would show me how!"

Sonny Boy blushed. He began to say that he was not much for spelling and fractions himself, but Lena touched his foot.

"Spelling and fractions are nothing! I'll show you how to do them," said Sonny Boy stoutly.

"And you'll show me how to straighten my legs, so I can be a soldier, won't you?" said Otto. 63

Sonny Boy moved about uneasily on his bow-legs. "It's queer! I want to be a soldier, too," he said. "Yes, I'll show you, Otto."

"You're what I've been wanting—a well boy!" said Otto, with a happy sigh. "You're very bright and clever, aren't you?"

"Oh, no," began Sonny Boy, but Lena touched his foot again.

"The Plummers are called a smart family," said Sonny Boy firmly, although his cheeks burned. "My brother Tom and my sister Trixie are very clever."

"Of course you couldn't have trained those mice if you hadn't been very clever," said Otto.

"Those mice have done him good. I've never seen him so bright," whispered the matron. "They've done all the children good!" 64

"And although I went away off to Uncle Fritz's to get the parrot for him, he says he doesn't like a parrot," whispered Lena.

"You like a parrot, don't you?" said Otto, eagerly, to Sonny Boy.

"I never was very well acquainted with one before. I think this one has a fine voice," said Sonny Boy politely.

"You like her better than you do the mice, don't you? You'll swap, won't you?" said Otto.

Now this, thought Sonny Boy, was hard! And what would they say at home? Trixie herself had trained the big mouse with the black spots on his ears that they called Admiral Cervera, and Tom would never be willing that Hobson should go out of the family!

"'JUST THINK! HE NEVER HAS HAD ONE GOOD TIME.'"

But Sonny Boy's heart ached with pity for the poor, humpbacked, shrunken fellow, whose face looked like a little old man's. And Lena leaned over Sonny Boy's shoulder and whispered:

"Just think! He never has had one good time!" she said.

"You can have them!" said Sonny Boy, although he had to swallow a great lump in his throat.

He got away as soon as he could then, for fear he should cry, Otto making him promise that he would come again just as soon as he could.

The delightful little glow at Sonny Boy's heart, such as you always feel when you have made any one happy, was queerly mixed with the grief of losing his white mice.

When he got to the entrance door he found that Polly had been shut up in a dark closet, because she whooped 68 and shouted so that the boy in buttons had not been able to keep her out upon the grounds.

When Sonny Boy took her again into his arms and started to go back, just as he had come away, he almost wished that Aunt Kate had borrowed some other one of the Plummers! 69

SONNY BOY BECOMES A SCHOLAR

71

CHAPTER V

SONNY BOY BECOMES A SCHOLAR

Polly was so lively on the way back to the city that Sonny Boy didn't dare to take her into a passenger-car. The smoking-car happened to be almost empty, and the conductor said he would better go in there.

Polly didn't like the empty smoking-car. She wished to be where there were plenty of people to admire her, and she showed her displeasure by making a dreadful noise. She barked and miaowed and cackled and crowed, and squealed and lowed and whinneyed and brayed and squawked and roared and growled, until one would have thought the smoking-car was 72 nothing less than Noah's Ark. A crowd of people came rushing into the car, and among them was a man who looked like a sailor, who insisted upon taking the covering from Polly's cage and holding her up to the light.

"Belong to you?" he said. "Don't want to sell her, do you?"

Sonny Boy's heart gave a great leap. He was himself so very tired of Polly's voice, and he had so dreaded to take her back to Aunt Kate, that it did not seem to him possible that any one could want her.

"She's a handsome bird," continued the man, "and hasn't she got a voice! She isn't exactly the bird for a home pet, but at a show she'd draw. And I belong to a show."

The man seated himself beside Sonny Boy and spoke in a low tone. "'The Wonder of the World'—that's 73 the name of the show that I belong to," he said.

That was the very circus that had been at Poppleton the summer before, the one that Tom had been so much interested in!

"Oh, then, perhaps you know all about the Wild Man of Borneo!" cried Sonny Boy eagerly. "Have you ever seen him *near to*?"

The sailor looked confused, and there was a queer twinkle in his eye.

"I am some acquainted with the Wild Man," he said slowly.

"Did he really come from Borneo? And is he truly wild?" asked Sonny Boy with eager curiosity.

"He is just about as wild as they make them," said the man, wagging his head solemnly. And Sonny Boy's heart thrilled with fear and wonder.

"We tried to play Wild Man in 74 our barn," he said to the man. "But none of the fellows knew how to be wild. Tom wanted me to find out how."

The sailor drew near to Sonny Boy and lowered his voice to a whisper. "It wouldn't do to let everybody know it, but if you and I are going to make a bargain about that parrot I don't care if I tell you that I'm the Wild Man of Borneo, and I'll show you just how I do it! I'll give you twenty dollars for the parrot, and I'll throw in the Wild Man business! I'll do more than that—I'll get you a chance to ride on the buffalo, in the procession, when the show comes to Bolton, this summer!"

Bolton was the town where the hospital was—the town they had just left. It would be easy to get to Bolton to the show.

"'I'LL GIVE YOU TWENTY DOLLARS FOR THE PARROT.'"

Twenty dollars might be a small price for the parrot, but the secret of being a Wild Man and the chance to ride on a buffalo were extras that a boy could not easily resist! The parrot changed hands, and so did two ten-dollar bills. And the man gave Sonny Boy his address so that he might find him when the show came to Bolton.

"Aren't you stuck up? Scat!" screamed Polly after Sonny Boy, by way of good-bye, when they parted at the city station.

Sonny Boy was very penitent when he found, on reaching home, that his absence had made Aunt Kate very anxious. She said a dreadful thing; she said that she never could trust Sonny Boy again!

But Sonny Boy knew she would find out that he wasn't the kind of a 78 boy that runs away. He thought it was enough to make any boy lose his mind to change his white mice for that parrot!

Aunt Kate thought that twenty dollars was a plenty for the parrot! She said she would see about the extras. She didn't seem to understand the advantages of learning to be a Wild Man or of riding on a buffalo.

But she said she thought of taking a house at Bolton for the summer, while her husband was away at the war; it was seashore, and it was also near the city, where she could hear the war-news soon.

And then Sonny Boy felt sure that he should not miss his extra pay for the parrot.

His sister Polly would not think that a boy ought to want to ride on a buffalo; she would say that none of 79 the Plummers had ever done such a thing. But Aunt Kate was different.

"There are other things I want, Aunt Kate," said Sonny Boy suddenly, and he stood as tall as he could before his aunt—so tall that his shoulders scarcely stooped and his bow-legs were almost straight. "I've got to have them!" Sonny Boy's red cheeks grew quite pale and his voice was gruff with feeling.

"Why, Sonny Boy dear, what can the things be that you want so much!" said Aunt Kate wonderingly.

"Spelling and fractions," said Sonny Boy firmly.

"You dear boy! I never heard of a boy who thought so much of his lessons as that!" exclaimed Aunt Kate.

"It's to show another fellow—stupider than I am," said Sonny Boy. "And crookeder. I've got to get 80 straight and be a soldier, too, to show him how." And he told her about Otto.

Aunt Kate hugged him and laughed a little and cried a little. And she said it was a beautiful idea and he should have a tutor so that he could learn spelling and fractions very fast. And he should go to a gymnasium and straighten his shoulders and his legs. And his uncle would take him to camp to see the soldiers drill.

And she would buy him some more white mice. But that last offer Sonny Boy declined. He wanted no white mice but those! And he didn't want those, because he liked better to have Otto and the poor invalid children have them.

It was quite wonderful to see how Sonny Boy learned spelling and fractions. The tutor was surprised, and 81 what the Poppleton schoolmistress would have thought no one can even guess! For Sonny Boy had been dull at his lessons.

And presently he straightened himself out in the most surprising way, and learned to drill soldiers like a major. He had a fine military company, in the "almost well" room of the children's ward at the hospital. The officers sent word to Aunt Kate that he was a very welcome visitor and did the children great good.

He bought a drum and fife with the parrot money, and sent them to the Poppleton Guards, the company to which "the fellows didn't want him to belong." And he wrote a letter to the Guards, telling them about the military tactics that he had learned at the camp, where his uncle had taken him. 82

"How quickly you have learned!" said Aunt Kate one day. "You are the very brightest one of the Plummers."

But Sonny Boy shook his head. "I never could learn until 'twas for another fellow," he said.

"Anyway, you're the dearest one of the Plummers!" said Aunt Kate, with a hug. By this time they were at Bolton for the summer, and they awoke one morning to find the place gay with show-bills and huge placards.

The "Wonder of the World" was coming to town. Among the attractions were the "Wild Man of Borneo," fresh from his native jungles, and "The Monster Tuscarora," the greatest buffalo in the world.

"'HOW QUICKLY YOU HAVE LEARNED,' SAID AUNT KATE."

That was the buffalo that he was to ride in the procession! Sonny Boy felt that even Polly ought to understand that this was a very great honor to come to one of the Plummers! 87

WHO WAS CAPTAIN OF THE COMPANY?

89

CHAPTER VI

WHO WAS CAPTAIN OF THE COMPANY?

The great show, the "Wonder of the World," had come to town. It came in the night and packed itself away in the big tents on Lawton's field.

A "monster street procession" was announced for the next morning, and the Bolton boys and girls lay awake as if it were the Fourth of July.

Sonny Boy had received a large square ticket, marked "Season," and "Complimentary," and in the same envelope was a slip of paper on which was written, "*Ask for J. Simpkins at the door.*" 90

J. Simpkins was, of course, Sonny Boy's friend, the Wild Man.

Aunt Kate said she felt doubtful about "that Wild Man business," and she wrote to her husband about it.

"It won't do him any harm to learn to be a Wild Man." That was Uncle William's answer; and Sonny Boy thought he was a very sensible man.

Aunt Kate also wrote to Mamma Plummer about the Wild Man and the buffalo, although she didn't tell Sonny Boy of that. And Mamma Plummer answered, "Sonny Boy could never learn to be a wild man; the dear boy is so quiet. And he would be scared to death at the sight of a buffalo."

Mamma Plummer did not quite understand her Sonny Boy.

"OTTO HAD HIS ONE GOOD TIME."

93

Sonny Boy asked for J. Simpkins at the tent door, showing his bit of paper, and he was told to follow a porter straight to the cage of the most ferocious-looking Wild Man that ever was seen!

He had horns, and he had tusks, and a mane like a horse, and yet when he laughed, Sonny Boy could see, as plainly as could be, that he was only the sailor who had bought the parrot!

If one could only be a Wild Man like that, in their barn at Poppleton, thought Sonny Boy, what fun it would be!

But there was no time to take a lesson in being a Wild Man this morning, as the procession was to start soon. And it happened that the boy who rode the buffalo was ill with the mumps, so they really needed another boy.

And the buffalo boy's scarlet and gold-laced tunic and trousers were an 94 exact fit for Sonny Boy, who looked quite straight and handsome in them!

That buffalo was such a huge beast that Sonny Boy had to mount him by means of a step-ladder. He was bigger than any geography buffalo you ever saw. And he tossed his horned head and pawed the ground with his great hoofs in a way that made Sonny Boy's heart go pit-a-pat.

But there was no outward sign that Sonny Boy's heart was going pit-a-pat. He was not going to miss the proudest moment of his life because he was afraid! When he rode out into the crowded street, the huge buffalo following after the troops of tiny Shetland ponies, the better to show his size, and the crowd shouted and cheered, if Sonny Boy did for a little while forget even Otto it was not strange!
95

But Otto did not allow himself to be forgotten. He wanted to see that procession with his own eyes. He had lain awake all night thinking about it. When the hospital supply-wagon was at the gate in the morning he watched his chance to slip out unobserved, and climbed into the back of the wagon!

It hurt him so that his white face grew whiter and there were drops on his forehead. He broke one of his crutches, too, and the other fell out of the wagon. But he was not found out! The driver was in a hurry, perhaps because he wished to see the procession himself. He jumped into the front of the wagon, without a glance at the back, and off down the hill rattled the wagon, with Otto in the back, in his dressing-gown, with a hospital blanket pinned over his shoulders.

Just as the hospital wagon reached 96 the procession the band struck up and the horse was frightened and jumped. It gave the wagon just enough of a jerk to throw Otto out. He was tossed into the little space between the ponies and the buffalo. The beast's great hoofs were almost upon him!

There was a wild cry from the crowd, but it was Sonny Boy who slipped from his high perch and, not an instant too soon, drew his friend out of the danger.

Sonny Boy lost his own footing; the buffalo's hoof grazed his arm and tore the gold lace of his tunic.

Friendly hands were ready to lift him again to his seat, while the crowd cheered him until it was hoarse.

"Otto first! Lift him up here and I will hold him on. It's his first good time." The marshal of the procession 97 made no objection, since it was something that pleased the crowd.

Up went Otto, in his blanket, to the front place, frightened, but not hurt, and Sonny Boy held him securely, and the crowd went wild!

Above all its noise a shrill voice suddenly came to Sonny Boy's ears.

"Cock-a-doodle-doo! Aren't you stuck up?"

And if there wasn't Polly, in a great gilt cage, swinging high above the Fat Lady's chariot!

Polly had been calling out the names of all the wonders in the show, as she had been taught, but when she saw Sonny Boy she remembered old times. She shouted out all the patriotism she knew, and the band played Yankee Doodle, and the people said that the best was what was not down in the bills. 98

Otto had his one good time! One would scarcely have known him, his face was so bright and rosy.

It was almost a miracle that he had not been killed under the buffalo's hoofs, but the ride did not hurt him in the least. And he is still telling the hospital children, over and over again, all the wonders of that procession in which he rode to the end of the route on the buffalo, and then back to the tent in the Fat Lady's chariot! For Sonny Boy found the Wild Man both a kind and influential friend.

He has learned to be a Wild Man himself; there was a show in the Plummers' barn, at Poppleton, in the fall, that many people thought equal to a grown-up circus, and the Wild Man was the chief attraction.

But none of the Plummers were so much surprised that Sonny Boy had learned to be a Wild Man as they were that he had learned spelling and fractions and straightened out his stooping shoulders and his bow-legs!

Sonny Boy explained that he had done it to help a slower and a crookeder boy than himself. And when Otto came down to Poppleton to pay Sonny Boy a visit they understood a little better.

Lena came, too, and they brought the white mice, and those skillful performers took part in the barn show.

Sonny Boy and Otto still think there was nothing in the "Wonder of the World" to beat those white mice.

Within a week after he returned to Poppleton, Tom told Sonny Boy that if he would only join the Guards as the fellows wanted him to he would surely be chosen captain!

"It would sound well—'Captain 102 Sonny Boy Plummer, of the Poppleton Guards,'" said Tom. And when I last heard from Poppleton that was what Sonny Boy was called—Captain Sonny Boy Plummer, of the Poppleton Guards!

And every one of the Plummers was wishing to be the one that Aunt Kate would borrow next.

And in a little while none of them remembered that they had ever thought it queer that Aunt Kate wanted to borrow Sonny Boy!

[THE END]